# RAISINS AND ALMONDS

## A Yiddish Lullaby

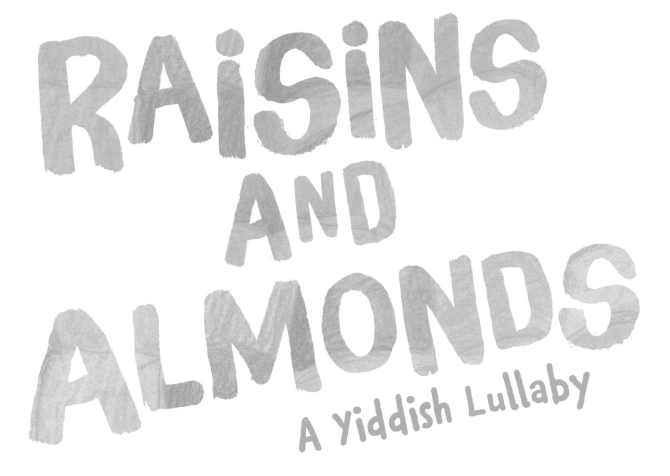

For my mother, who sang this song,
and for the new generation of listeners,
Mairenie, Ana, Juliet, and Alex — S.T.

For Teresa K, and my family — S. S.

Recording of "Raisins and Almonds" by
Yale Strom — director, violin. www.yalestrom.com
Elizabeth Schwartz — vocals, baritone, ukulele. www.voiceofklezmer.com
Luke Jungers — camera, sound, edit. www.cuttingroomfloor.com

KAR-BEN PUBLISHING, INC.
A division of Lerner Publishing Group, Inc.
241 First Avenue North
Minneapolis, MN 55401 USA
1-800-4-KARBEN

Website address: www.karben.com

Main body text set in Mikado Medium
Typeface provided by HVD Fonts

**Library of Congress Cataloging-in-Publication Data**
Names: Tarcov, Susan, author. | Sánchez, Sonia, 1983- illustrator.
Title: Raisins and almonds : a Yiddish lullaby / by Susan Tarcov ; illustrated by
    Sonia Sanchez.
Description: Minneapolis : Kar-Ben Publishing, [2019] | Summary: Although she
    does not want to leave her mother's warm bed, Annie decides to visit the store
    under her bed, run by a little white goat, and meets fellow shoppers along the
    way. Includes notes about the original folk song.
Identifiers: LCCN 2018011878 (print) | LCCN 2018018311 (ebook) |
    ISBN 9781541542167 (eb pdf) | ISBN 9781541521612 (lb : alk. paper) |
    ISBN 9781541521629 (pb : alk. paper)
Subjects: | CYAC: Shopping—Fiction. | Animals—Fiction. | Imagination—Fiction. |
    Jews—Fiction. | Lullabies—Fiction.
Classification: LCC PZ7.1.T38314 (ebook) | LCC PZ7.1.T38314 Rai 2019 (print) |
    DDC [E]—dc23

LC record available at https://lccn.loc.gov/2018011878

Manufactured in the United States of America
1-44388-34649-6/19/2018

# RAISINS AND ALMONDS

## A Yiddish Lullaby

Susan Tarcov

illustrated by Sonia Sánchez

KAR-BEN
PUBLISHING

***Scribble-scrabble.*** The noise came from under Bella's bed. ***Scribble-scrabble.*** What could it be?

Bella ran to her mama's
bed. "Mama! There's
something under my bed!"

"Don't worry," her mama
said. "It's just a little white goat."

Bella climbed into her mama's bed.
Just a little white goat, what a relief!
"Why is he there?" she asked.

"His little store is there, under your bed," her mama said.

"What does he sell?" Bella asked.

"You never know. You'll have to go and see."

Should Bella go? It was so nice and warm in her mama's bed.

"Will he have a red bicycle?" she asked.

"You never know," her mama said.

"Will he have a green bicycle helmet with a dinosaur on it?"

"You never know," her mama said.

"Will he have a necklace like the one my Bubbe has?"

"You'll have to go and see."

Bella still couldn't decide. It seemed like such a long way back to her room. And she was barefoot. Her feet would get cold.

She put down one foot. The floor wasn't cold. She put down the other foot. It wasn't the floor at all, it was grass!

"WHERE ARE YOU GOING?" asked a tiny voice. It was a mouse peeking out of his mouse hole.

"I'm going to the little white goat's store under my bed," Bella said. "Would you like to come?"

"WILL HE HAVE A TINY TABLE AND CHAIRS?" he asked.

"You never know," Bella said.

"WILL HE HAVE A TINY BED FOR ME?"

"You never know," Bella said.

"WILL HE HAVE A TINY MEZUZAH FOR MY DOORPOST?"

"Why don't you come and see?"

The mouse went with Bella across the grass.
Now Bella had a friend to keep her company.

**"WHERE ARE YOU GOING?"**

asked a medium-size voice.
A fuzzy rabbit was planting
seeds in the ground.

"We're going to the little white goat's store under my bed," Bella said. "Would you like to come?"

The rabbit looked at his row of seeds.

## "WILL HE HAVE A WATERING CAN?" he asked.

"You never know," Bella said.

# "WILL HE HAVE A RED WHEELBARROW?"

"You never know," Bella said.

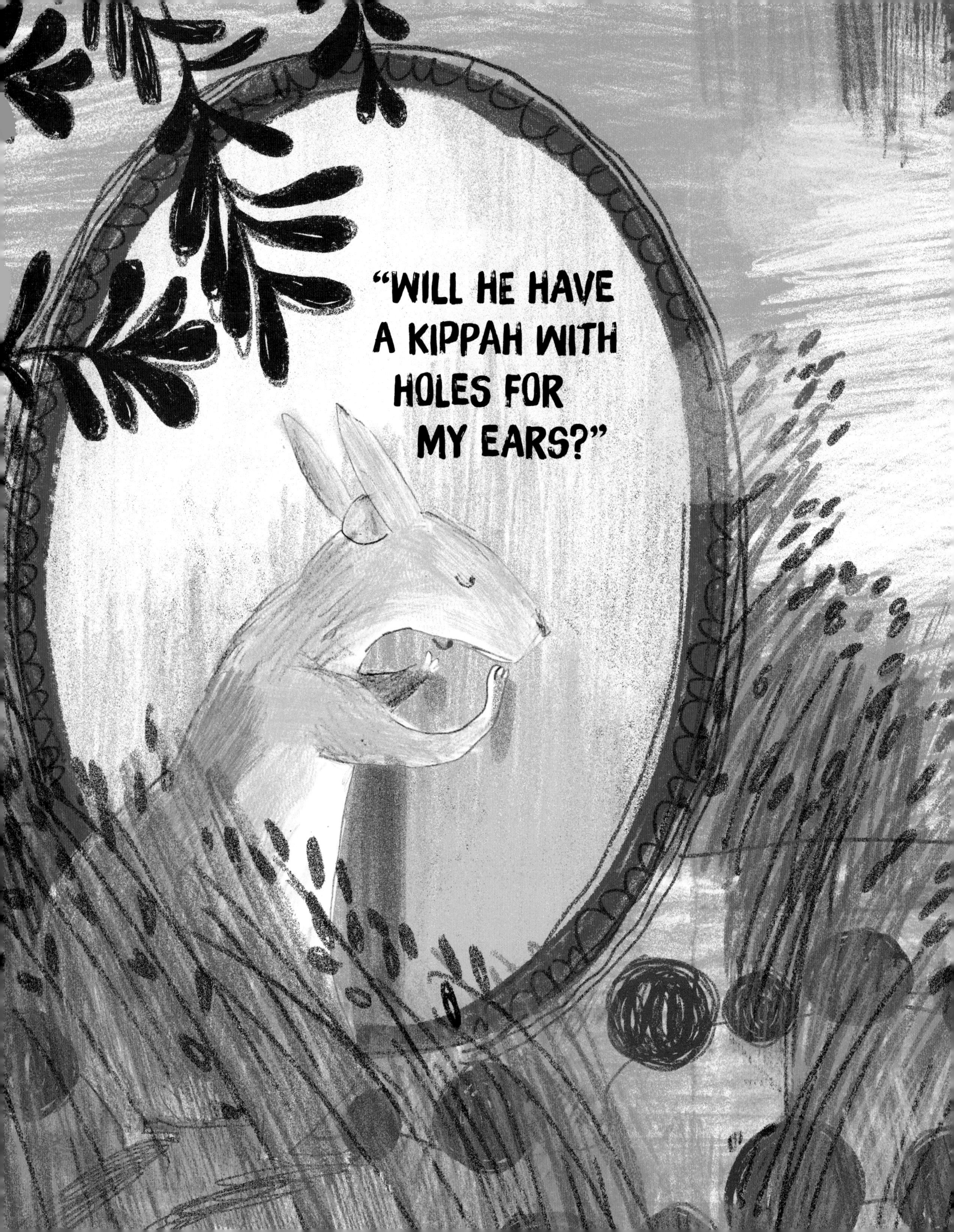

"WILL HE HAVE A KIPPAH WITH HOLES FOR MY EARS?"

"Why don't you come and see?"

The rabbit went with Bella and the mouse. The three friends skipped along happily.

**"WHERE ARE YOU GOING?"**

asked a great big voice. A big-eyed wolf was hiding at the edge of the woods.

"We're going to the little white goat's store under my bed," Bella said. "Would you like to come?"

The wolf's stomach growled.

## "WILL HE HAVE PICKLED HERRING?"

he asked.

"You never know," Bella said.

"WILL HE HAVE
BAGELS AND LOX?"

"You never know," Bella said.

"WILL HE HAVE PASTRAMI SANDWICHES?"

"You'll have to come and see."

The wolf went with Bella and her friends.

The wolf's talk of food had made them all hungry.

They crossed a brook.

They came to a clearing among the trees.

And there he was! The little white goat was standing under Bella's bed!

What was he selling?

RAISINS
AND
ALMONDS.

## AUTHOR'S NOTE

"Raisins and Almonds" is a well-known and much loved Yiddish lullaby. The most famous version of this song comes from the operetta *Shulamis*, written in 1881 by Abraham Goldfaden. Goldfaden adapted his version of the song's chorus from the melody and poetry of a 19th century Eastern European Yiddish folk song.

It tells the story of a snowy white goat that travels to market selling his wares, trading in raisins and almonds. Raisins and almonds were some of the most luxurious things one could imagine in the old Jewish communities of Eastern Europe.

### "ROZHINKES MIT MANDLEN"
### LYRICS BY ABRAHAM GOLDFADEN

*Unter Yidele's vigele*
*Shteyt a klor-vays tsigele*
*Dos tsigele iz geforn handlen*
*Dos vet zayn dayn baruf*
*Rozhinkes mit mandlen*
*Slof-zhe, Yidele, shlof.*

### "RAISINS AND ALMONDS"

*To my little one's cradle in the night*
*Comes a little goat snowy and white*
*The goat will trot to the market*
*While mother her watch does keep*
*Bringing back raisins and almonds*
*Sleep, my little one, sleep.*

*Scan the QR code to watch musicians Yale Strom and Elizabeth Schwartz perform the song "Rozhinkes Mit Mandlen" that inspired this story.*
*http://www.karben.com/raisinsandalmonds*